A JOB FOR
WITTILDA

by Caralyn and Mark Buehner

DIAL BOOKS FOR YOUNG READERS New York

Published by Dial Books for Young Readers
A Division of Penguin Books USA Inc.
375 Hudson Street · New York, New York 10014

Library of Congress Cataloging in Publication Data
Buehner, Caralyn.
A job for Wittilda / by Caralyn Buehner; pictures by Mark Buehner.
p. cm.
Summary: When Wittilda the witch is forced to look for a job,
she finds her broom-flying ability comes in handy in
applying for a job delivering pizzas.
ISBN 0-8037-1149-2 (trade).—ISBN 0-8037-1150-6 (lib. bdg.)
[1. Witches—Fiction. 2. Work—Fiction. 3. Pizza—Fiction.]
I. Buehner, Mark, ill. II. Title.
PZ7.B884Jo 1993 [E]—dc20 91-15630 CIP AC

*The art for this book was prepared by
using oil paints over acrylics.*

To Mom Morris, whose cupboards are always full,
and Dad Morris, who dries everything (except rats).
C.B. and M.B.

There were cats on the table, cats on the chairs, cats on the sofa, the bookshelves, the stairs!

Every half-starved stray, every unwanted kitten seemed to find its way into Wittilda's heart and kitchen.

Wittilda loved them all.

But...it *was* getting hard to feed them. They didn't like bat-wing stew or roast newt, which was all Wittilda could cook, and the mice had long since disappeared.

"We're down to our last dried rat," Wittilda worried.

"Meow?" the cats queried. *"Marroow?"*

"There's only one thing to do," Wittilda decided. "I'll have to get a job. I'll go and talk to Aunt Bort. Maybe I can work for her!"

Wittilda kissed forty-seven soft noses and set off for Aunt Bort's Hair Palace.

Eventually Aunt Bort was persuaded to hire Wittilda.

"Please comb Mrs. Hatrack's hair," Aunt Bort grunted.

Wittilda began to comb. How boring, she thought, I can do better than that.

Mrs. Hatrack's wispy hair reminded Wittilda of spider threads. She began tying knots here and there, and soon Mrs. Hatrack's hair fanned out in an enormous web.

"*Hmmmmmmm.* Something's missing," Wittilda murmured. Reaching deep in her pocket, she pulled out a small black spider and placed it carefully in the web of hair.

"Don't move," she cautioned. Mrs. Hatrack and the spider held very still. Wittilda sprayed the web with hair spray until it glistened.

"Beautiful!" she exclaimed.

Mrs. Hatrack looked up from her magazine.

"*EEEEEEEEEEEEEEEEEE! EEEEEEEEEEEEEEEEEEEE!*"
she screamed.

"WITTILDA!" Aunt Bort thundered, "WHAT HAVE YOU DONE?"

"I think it's pretty," Wittilda said defensively.
"YOU'RE FIRED!" shouted Aunt Bort.

Glumly Wittilda shuffled home.
"I got fired," she told the cats.
"Hsssssssssssssssssssssssssssssssssssss!"
They were all very hungry that day.

Wittilda searched the job ads in the newspaper.

Carpenter? Secretary? Exterminator?

"Rats," muttered Wittilda. Then her eyes lit up as she read:

DELIVERY PERSON WANTED EVENINGS.
Must have own transportation.
Apply in person at Dingaling Pizza.

"It's perfect!" she cackled.

Wittilda blew forty-seven kisses, grabbed her broom, and ran out. She skidded to a stop at Dingaling's and waited nervously with the other applicants.

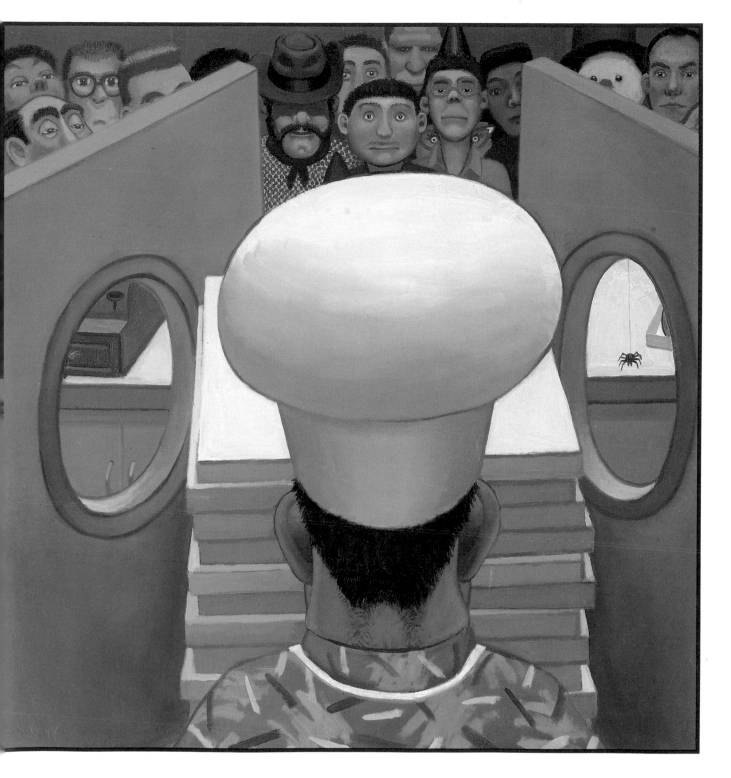

Suddenly the door burst open. Out came Joe Dingaling, his arms loaded with boxes.

"Here you go," barked Joe. "Five pizzas each to deliver. The first one back gets the job!"

Arms and legs flew as everyone grabbed a stack of pizzas and raced away.

Wittilda mounted her broom and chanted:

Notions and potions, buzzard stew,
Curdle a girdle with rattlesnake glue.
Rickety, rackety, my one green eye,
Loomity, Broomity, time to fly!

Wittilda shot up into the night. She dipped and swooped
through the air to the first house on her list.

Mrs. Pink was surprised to get her pizza so soon.
"Extraordinary!" she fluttered, counting out money for
the pizza.

Wittilda whizzed around the block to the Muzzles', down
the street to the Zippits', then flew across town to Mr. Boney's.

She knocked and knocked. Finally Mr. Boney came to the door.

"Thank you," he whispered, dropping the money penny by penny into Wittilda's hand. Wittilda danced from foot to foot.

At last she was on her way.

"I'm making great time," she exclaimed. "I'm going to win!"

As she was rising up in the air, Wittilda heard a tiny sound. Silently she hovered.

"*Merrerouw!*"

Anxiously Wittilda peered around. A bit of white, high in a tree, caught her eye.

"Oh, the poor little thing!"

Just then a motorcycle roared around the corner. It was one of the people trying for the job at Dingaling's!

"Oh, what shall I do?" Wittilda agonized. "If I stop to help the kitten, someone else will get back to Dingaling's before me. I'll come back later...."

She began to glide away.

"*Merrerouw!*"

"Wait! I'm coming!" shouted Wittilda. "Don't move!"

Wittilda scrambled onto a low branch. Twigs snagged at her clothes and caught in her hair as she crawled upward.

"Merrerouw!"

The kitten stared at Wittilda with wide, scared eyes.

"Here, kitty-kitty!" Wittilda reached up. "Come here, baby."

Inch by inch the kitten eased toward her.

As Wittilda reached out to grab the kitten, a sudden gust of
wind shook the tree. Wittilda and the kitten plummeted head
over heels to the ground below.

"Are you all right?" Wittilda asked.

"Reeoorrrrr!"

"Then let's go!"

Luckily, at the last house, Mrs. Noodle was knitting on the front porch. Wittilda tossed the pizza box onto her lap.

"Here's your pizza!" she cried, and snatching the money from a dazed Mrs. Noodle, Wittilda spun around and headed back to Dingaling's.

Wittilda had never flown so fast.

The wind whipped her hair and cloak.

Seconds later she stumbled breathlessly into Dingaling's.

Joe's mouth dropped open.
"How did you do it? It's only been fifteen minutes!"
Wittilda's eyes danced as Joe slapped her on the back.
"The job is yours!" cried Joe. "Here, have some pizza!"

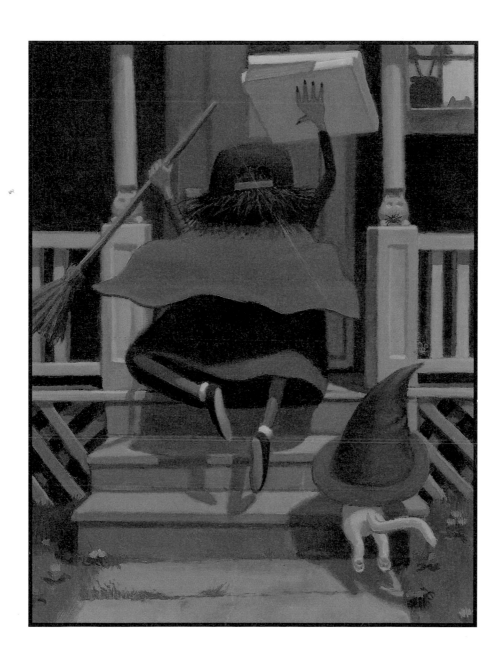

That night Wittilda tripped lightly up her front steps and opened the door.

"I'm home!" she sang. "I got the job!"

"*Prrrrrrrrrrrrrrrrrrrrrrrrr! Prrrrrrrrrrrrrrrr!*" Forty-eight cats tried to rub against her legs.

"I just love it! And . . ." Wittilda set the Dingaling special
combo down on the table . . . "you're going to love it too!"

And they did.